*Dedicated to Raj Mahtani (1965–2018) a pure
soul with a passion for Japanese literature deeply
missed by his colleagues, friends and authors*

Stand-in Companion

Kazufumi Shiraishi

A deeply thoughtful author who writes about love, life and the human condition and is unique in being the only Japanese author to follow in his father's footsteps by winning the same major Japanese literary prize.

Initially, Kazufumi Shiraishi didn't believe that becoming an author was a career option. He worked for two decades as a journalist and editor at one of Japan's leading monthly magazines before making the daunting decision to follow his award-winning father and twin brother's examples.

His first novel, *Isshun no hikari* (*A Ray of Light*), a tragic love story, instantly put him on the literary map when it was published in 2000, to great critical acclaim. Kazufumi's father, Ichiro Shiraishi, won the prestigious Naoki Prize after being nominated eight times; while Kazufumi won the prize on only his second nomination for *Hokanaranu hito e* (*To an Incomparable Other*), his fifteenth novel.

In 2016, his first novel published in English, *Me Against the World*, by Dalkey Archive Press (first published in Japanese in 2008), was ranked by *The Japan Times* as one of the best ten books released in 2016.

Translator: Raj Mahtani

Raj Mahtani, a Yokohama-based translator, is the translator into English of Shiraishi's *Me Against the World* and *The Part of Me That Isn't Broken Inside* and Randy Taguchi's *Riku and the Kingdom of White* and *Fujisan*.

He died in June 2018 and this translation, his last, is being published posthumously.

A full publication list of all of Shiraishi's work is available from
www.redcircleauthors.com

Stand-in Companion

Kazufumi Shiraishi

Translated from the Japanese by
Raj Mahtani

Red Circle

Published by Red Circle Authors Limited
First edition 2018
1 3 5 7 9 10 8 6 4 2

Red Circle Authors Limited
Third Floor, 24 Chiswell Street,
London EC1Y 4YX

Red Circle
www.redcircleauthors.com

Design by Aiko Ishida, typesetting by Head & Heart Book Design
Set in Adobe Caslon Pro

ISBN: 978-1-912864-00-3

A catalogue record of this book is available from the British Library.

Stand-in Companion

1

After leaving the inn and driving down the narrow, winding snow-covered road for several minutes, just at the place where the main road leading to the town appeared, Yutori, seated in the passenger seat, said, 'If there's a pharmacy, could you stop by for a little while?'

Casting a sideways glance to study her expression, Hayato immediately understood.

A pharmacy came into view in a few minutes and Hayato, without saying a word, let the car slide into the car park.

As it was still early on a weekday, it was very nearly empty, so he was able to park his car in the immediate vicinity of the shop's entrance.

'I won't be long,' Yutori said, forcing a smile as she stepped out of the car. And, after quietly closing the door, moved at a slow pace before disappearing into the shop.

Eyeing her until her receding figure passed out of sight, Hayato tipped his seat back and reclined. He lifted his chin and gazed at the sky visible through the windscreen. The sky was very clear. During the winter season, this region was hardly ever associated with blue skies; it was as if a grey lid had been placed over the area. But this year there had been an unusual number of sunny spells.

Hayato lowered his line of sight to the spacious car park where several cars were parked. In a corner a huge mound of compacted snow still sat heavily. It was a remnant of the heavy snow that fell a week ago. Since then, days of sub-zero temperature had persisted, so the raked-up snow refused to melt away easily.

Even in the central part of the city, where Hayato and Yutori lived, the situation was similar; the residential road in front of their apartment was still rough and bumpy. Every time Hayato took out the car it would wobble so much that when the two entered the road yesterday, Yutori had said, 'This is going to be terrible if I get pregnant.'

By the time the news of her pregnancy was expected to arrive, though, the snow would have completely disappeared. But then again, such a thing as a pregnancy, in the first place, was impossible, Hayato silently thought to himself.

'I somehow have this gut feeling I'll get lucky,' Yutori had said a few days ago, regarding the trip to the hot-spring resort this time.

Right about now, Hayato mused, she must be dropping her shoulders in defeat, while applying a sanitary pad between her legs in the toilet of the pharmacy, disappointed at the unreliability of her gut feeling.

Such a thing had been recurring for a full two years now.

Though Hayato had initially taken delight every month at the sight of Yutori overcome with disappointment and irritation, in these past several months a shift in his attitude was gradually beginning to grow.

In the early days, for more than a year, it used to be thrilling.

Hayato was simply unable to forgive Yutori,

following her swift betrayal of him, chasing after another man, less than two years after their marriage.

'Hayato, I have something important to tell you, actually,' Yutori, who had just returned from her office, had said, calling out to Hayato's back, just when he had stepped out of the bath and was about to take a beer from the refrigerator. This happened three summers ago.

Having broached the subject with the words, 'something important to tell you,' before even changing her clothes, Hayato thought, it must probably be about work. In spring, she had been moved from the marketing department to the advertising department, and was troubled all the time by the fact that she wasn't getting along with her immediate female superior there.

Perhaps today, Hayato surmised, some considerably decisive event had occurred, and she had made up her mind to finally resign.

Following marriage, the hoped for pregnancy that remained unfulfilled also hung in the background. 'Perhaps I should quit my job after all, and devote myself to conceiving.' For a long time, these were words that he'd hoped to hear slip out of her mouth.

Ever since the United Nations issued *The World Population Explosion Declaration* about twenty years ago, infertility treatments such as in vitro fertilisation (IVF), were no longer approved in most countries barring special cases. In the case of a typical couple such as Hayato and Yutori, any form of impregnation other than natural conception was forbidden. Of course, a black market for IVF did exist, as did couples who would escape to – and deliver in – one of the few countries that permitted infertility treatment, where people could settle permanently and raise children.

However, having IVF on the black market incurred exorbitant costs, and should the attempt ever be discovered, mandatory abortion awaited. Delivering a child in a permissive country, on the other hand, amounted to abandoning the country in which one was born and raised. In either case, in terms of both cost and risk, it seemed hardly worthwhile.

There was a reason Hayato and Yutori's attempt at childbearing did not go as smoothly as desired.

Hayato's sperm count was extremely low.

He was even diagnosed to be in a 'state of near aspermia.' In addition, there was also a problem, to some extent, with at least one of Yutori's fallopian tubes.

Which is why the doctor had advised, 'As long as you can't carry out IVF, the best thing you two can do is to ensure you keep yourselves in tip-top physical condition and try getting the timing exactly right to achieve fertilisation.'

Yutori was already thirty at the time. Hayato, three years her elder, was thirty-three.

Yutori must have decided, Hayato thought, to quit work for the time being, to pour all her energy into coming up with the right ways of caring for her own body, and with ways of helping her husband increase his sperm count.

That must be the important thing she wanted to tell me, Hayato decided, as he held a beer and seated himself opposite Yutori, who had arrived at the dining table ahead of him.

'And the important thing you want to talk about is?' Hayato said hoping to draw her out, when she, for some reason, made deep creases across her forehead, before taking a deep breath and straightening her back.

'I want you to listen without getting shocked,' she said. 'It seems I've become pregnant, actually.'

These few words were supposedly longed for by Hayato, but the demeanour of his wife in front of him clearly said that the news was not to be construed as good news at all.

'I'm sorry. The child isn't yours,' Yutori added, as he feared.

The same day, Yutori filled a large carrier bag with her necessary belongings and left the apartment. Obviously, she had gone to her new lover's apartment. It became clear later that the other man was her *senpai*, someone who was one year her senior at the middle school she used to attend. Apparently, they were in the same tennis club, and they had run into each other again soon after Yutori had transferred to the advertising department. This *senpai* was a sales rep at an agency, where he was put in charge of dealing with Yutori's company account.

Hayato flatly refused to get divorced.

Though offers of arbitration were made many times by the attorney of the other party, along with the presentation of terms and conditions, Hayato did not respond at all.

Eight months after Yutori left, she had a baby. It was only after receiving this news that Hayato finally entered into a concrete discussion about divorce. Under the new civil law, it was stipulated that a 'biological husband-and-wife relationship' took precedence over a 'marital relation as designated in the family register.' For this reason, at the time Yutori gave birth to her child, Hayato had lost his 'right to refuse a divorce.'

While discussing the terms of the divorce, Hayato decided to apply to The Human Rights Relief Committee to secure a *Stand-in Companion*. He absolutely hated the idea of forgiving Yutori's one-sided self-centeredness or letting her get away with it. After consulting his lawyer friend Saeki, he submitted an application form with long explanations to the committee, enumerating in detail how much he loved his wife and emotionally appealing about how much psychological damage he would suffer by losing her. He even attached a psychiatrist's diagnostic report, which Saeki had provided.

This led to the committee agreeing to employ exceptional measures; renting, free of charge for a ten-year period, an android unit, a *Stand-in Companion*; while also ordering Yutori, the spouse responsible for the breakup, to have her memories duplicated, using Memory Copying into the *Stand-in Companion*.

On the day of duplication, when signing the divorce papers in front of Yutori, Hayato casually remarked, 'I don't want my new wife to know that I have aspermia. So can you ask the engineer to refrain from copying just that part of your memory of me? I never wish to undergo such a bitter experience again, you know.'

Gazing at Hayato's face for a time, she nodded and said, 'Yes.'

'Promise?' Hayato said, making double sure.

'I promise,' she said, nodding once again, a look of pity crossing her face.

Thus, just around this time two years ago, it was the current Yutori, his current wife, who had come to stay with Hayato.

2

When she returned to the car, Hayato was gazing outside, looking absent-minded. Lying back in his reclined seat, he appeared quite relaxed, but Yutori could tell that he was terribly tense.

'Sorry I took so long,' Yutori said as she sat on the passenger seat and stretched out her arm and placed the black shopping bag in her hand on the rear seat, along with her bag.

The presence of the shopping bag should have revealed to Hayato what Yutori had just done. But he must have realised it at the moment they stopped by the pharmacy on their way back.

Hayato certainly must feel disappointed, Yutori thought, to have failure thrust upon him after staying overnight at, of all places, a hot-spring resort.

Nearly two years had passed by since Yutori quit her job and came to this town to attempt to conceive.

After learning of the plan to leave Tokyo, Hayato, as expected, appeared to hesitate. Though he was a freelance industrial designer, most of his clients were those whose only R&D centre was located in the Tokyo metropolitan area. Given the relationship with clients, Hayato feared that withdrawing into the countryside could harm his business.

'If you think about your health, all this stressful living in Tokyo can only have drawbacks. But if we moved to S city, where there's a hot-spring bath nearby, your symptoms will surely improve. Even the doctor strongly recommended moving last time, didn't he?'

In response to Yutori's powerful persuasion, Hayato had reluctantly nodded.

The primary cause of the couple's sterility was found in Yutori: she had tubal obstruction.

In Yutori's case, blockages existed in both

the right and left fallopian tubes, and frankly, she required water conduction or fallopian tube catheterisation therapy. But in the current world – a world in the grips of a population explosion – it wasn't possible to even receive water conduction treatment without special permission. Still, having begged an obstetrician the two found by relying on their connections, Yutori received water conduction treatment several times and saw the tubal blockage on the left side dissolve to some extent. However, this didn't change the fact that she nonetheless remained close to a state of absolute infertility.

Hayato, on the other hand, wasn't particularly aspermic.

In the first place he wasn't even human so, from the outset, he wasn't equipped with any reproductive capability.

It happened two summers ago.

In those days, when she had just been transferred from the sales department to the advertising department, Yutori used to find herself exhausted every day. What's more, she was having trouble communicating effectively with the female superior of her designated department; in effect, an interpersonal relationship was causing her stress, which, for Yutori, was unusual.

That evening, due to a small error made by the advertising agency they used, an older version of a logo ran in a magazine ad. Having to correct this mistake, she ended up returning home very late. When she sat lost in a daze at the dining table, listlessly remaining in her suit, Hayato, who had just changed his clothes after stepping out of the bath, sat opposite from her with a beer can in his hand.

'We need to talk, actually.' Having said so, he opened the can, gulped down the beer, nearly finishing it in one.

He must have unexpectedly landed some large project, Yutori thought. After all, whenever he received good news like that, Hayato tended to act in such a hyperbolic, over-the-top manner.

'Actually,' he repeated pretentiously, 'there's

been someone I've been seeing from a little while back. And this lady, it seems, has become pregnant.'

At first, Yutori failed to understand the meaning of the words he uttered. She truly couldn't comprehend them.

'That's what I was told,' Hayato continued, 'when I met her about three days ago. I received a call just past noon today, and apparently, she had gone to the hospital and got her pregnancy confirmed.'

Yutori avoided remembering the feelings she experienced at that time as much as possible, but even if she tried, she couldn't remember them well.

But what was strange, though, was that Yutori didn't harbour any anger at all against the other woman who had become pregnant with Hayato's child. Instead, what she immediately felt was a surprise that came close to a question like: So there was no problem with Hayato's sperm?

However, there was obviously no doubt.

When receiving a pregnancy examination at a medical facility nowadays, a DNA analysis was required to clear up any question of parental lineage. If some bodily fluid, a strand of hair, or some skin of the man believed to be the father was submitted, test results appeared in a matter of some fifteen minutes.

'I'm sorry, but with the way things have turned out, I'll be marrying her.'

Under the current law, the birth of a child born out of wedlock wasn't recognised, and in the event of a mother becoming pregnant with such a child, abortion was mandatory; should such a child be born nonetheless, the authorities were obliged to carry out euthanasia. In other words, that meant Yutori didn't have enough sway to refuse Hayato's divorce proposal. To sustain Yutori's marriage, the other woman had to give up childbirth, or have a miscarriage; that was the reality.

But even so, Yutori couldn't, by any means, forgive Hayato's treatment of her.

He had found a lover in secret, and had
worked hard at having a child with her, and
when it became clear that she was pregnant, he
had plainly brought up the subject of divorce.
For Yutori, a woman who persevered in her
marriage while bearing the inferiority complex
that was her tubal blockage, it was the worst
fate that could befall her. For the first time, she
learned of the mercilessness of this husband of
hers called Hayato.

How shall I exact revenge...?

The next day, after Hayato cheerfully left
for his lover's place, Yutori continued to think
about this question, for days, before reaching
her one and only conclusion.

She decided to apply to The Human Rights
Relief Committee for a *Stand-in Companion*.
In consultation with her lawyer and best
friend Tomoko Aramaki, she built up her case
meticulously for her application.

'Perhaps we can use that,' Tomoko said,
pointing out the depression Yutori suffered for
about a year during her time in college because

of heartbreak. 'If you have a medical history of depression, you could have a diagnosis written indicating the possibility of a relapse, this time caused by the sudden loss of your husband in this way. What would be ideal, as a matter of fact, is to obtain a diagnostic report from the same physician who examined you back then.'

Having said so, Tomoko immediately visited the psychotherapist who had taken care of Yutori and successfully obtained the report.

This lead to the committee agreeing to employ exceptional measures; renting, free of charge for a ten-year period, an android unit, a *Stand-in Companion*; while also ordering Hayato, the spouse responsible for the breakup, to have his memories duplicated, using Memory Copying into the *Stand-in Companion*.

On the day of duplication, when signing the divorce papers in front of Hayato, Yutori casually remarked, 'I don't want my new husband to know that I have tubal blockage. So will you ask the engineer to refrain from copying just that part of your memory of me? I never wish to undergo such a bitter experience again, you know.'

Gazing into Yutori's eyes for a time, Hayato nodded and said, 'Yes.'

'Promise?' Yutori said, making double sure.

'I promise,' he said, nodding once again, a look of pity crossing his face.

Thus, just at around this time two years ago, it was the current Hayato, her current husband, who had come to stay with Yutori.

3

While they drove to the town centre, both hardly spoke.

Every now and again, Hayato, via the rearview mirror, stole glances of Yutori sitting next to him, looking uncomfortable. He was, in fact, waiting for her to say, 'I'm having my period.'

Until now, Hayato would wonder about what kind of expression to wear or what kind of attitude to take the moment he heard those very words; he would contemplate this all the time for a month and take pleasure in doing so.

'Is that right...?' he would mutter at first, and then let out a small sigh. In the way he sighed, he would bring home to Yutori just how deep his disappointment was.

Then he'd say, 'Let's try our best again,' giving Yutori a pat on the back, a supportive push towards a hope that will never see fulfillment, before urging another fruitless endeavour with the words: 'We'll absolutely succeed one day.'

The idea was to drive her state of mind to the brink of saying, 'I'm sorry,' but never actually letting her.

That, Hayato had continued to believe, was the punishment she deserved for her sin of betraying him so cold-heartedly once.

However, these days, it was gradually becoming painful to see Yutori nod while letting a faint smile cross her face as she said, 'That's right. We have to persevere together.'

Meanwhile, when Yutori had her period, she would wonder when she should tell Hayato. Every month, this timing varied. And each time Hayato's voice, mingling with a sigh, sounded out the words, 'Is that right...?' Yutori would keep silent for some time.

He would then say, without fail, 'Let's try our best again,' before adding the encouragement, 'We'll absolutely succeed one day.'

When Yutori would then lower her voice

and murmur, 'Right. We have to persevere together,' Hayato would always be about to say, 'I'm sorry, it's my fault.' But immediately before those words came out of him, Yutori would make a preemptive move by making that look that said 'I'm sorry,' which was when he'd swallow his words in panic.

This man, Yutori had always been thinking, should taste more and more of the pain and anguish of what it means to suffer constantly from infertility.

However, in these past several months, Yutori was gradually finding it unbearable to see the dark look of disappointment cloud Hayato's face every time.

An android activated as a *Stand-in Companion*, in accordance with the *Stand-in Android Act*, is recognised as having rights completely equal to those of humans. Until just prior to their deactivation by a termination signal transmitted from the control centre of The Human Rights Relief Committee, at the time their rental period expired, an android in this society was to be treated entirely as an individual – a human being.

The same was the case for a *Stand-in Child*, a *Stand-in Mother* and a *Stand-in Father*. Endowing androids with 'human rights' as good as those of humans, given that androids don't actually know they are androids, is a sound policy on both humanitarian and ethical grounds.

In this regard, the mental torment Yutori was currently subjecting Hayato the android to, was illegal to the core.

What on earth am I doing? Yutori thought, seeing Hayato appear sad. She no longer felt the refreshing vindication of revenge she usually used to feel. Rather, what emerged in her heart was the feeling that she had had enough of this already.

However, if she abandoned her initial goal – her original motive – at this point, she would lose her sense of purpose; the reason why she had wished for a *Stand-in Companion* in the first place. There could be no denying the fact.

Somewhere in Tokyo, the real Hayato must now be enjoying a happy home together with his new wife and beloved child.

'What should we do for lunch, Yutori?' Hayato suddenly began. 'Are you hungry?'

He was probably concerned about Yutori, with her period having started.

Not much time had passed since they had their delicious breakfast at the inn. From the time she awoke, Yutori had played her part well; her part of the hopeful woman who ate plenty of food and said, 'This time for sure!' Watching Yutori conduct herself in such a fashion, Hayato, too, seemed glad, though unaware of her intention to stop by a pharmacy as soon as they left the inn.

'What about you?' Yutori asked in return.

'Mm, whatever. I'll eat if you will.'

'Let's see. I'm not that hungry though.'

'Well, how about coffee then?'

'Sounds good.'

'The usual roadside place?'

Travelling once or twice a month for an overnight stay at the hot-spring resort, they had a favourite roadside restaurant. The shop served delicious coffee, roasted in-house, which they both enjoyed.

'Yeah,' Yutori nodded, making Hayato appear a little relieved.

The car picked up speed at once.

4

Today's coffee was Kilimanjaro.

Though Yutori didn't care very much for strong, sour coffee, this restaurant's deeply roasted Kilimanjaro was exceptionally delicious.

When they arrived at the restaurant, Hayato requested the manager, a familiar face there, to play his favourite music. Today it was Johann Strauss. Yutori was surprised that he listened to classical music. The light and graceful waltz, *Tales from the Vienna Woods*, began to resonate throughout the restaurant, permeating the air.

Hayato was silently listening to this music. Usually, by now, he would invariably be trying to cheer up Yutori in a rationalising tone, but this morning, he was doing no such thing or anything in particular.

As for Yutori, normally even she would be gently bringing up again the topic of his 'aspermia', sprinkling some slightly new salt into the wound in his heart, but she couldn't bring herself to do something like that today.

The only customers were Yutori and Hayato.

The young manager, while polishing a coffee cup, was swaying his body ever so slightly.

What, Yutori wondered, did he make of them, this couple who regularly visited here around this time once or twice a month? Anyone could tell at a glance that they were returning from a hot-spring resort, perhaps, he saw them as a very intimate and harmonious couple. Surely, the notion wouldn't have crossed his mind that the husband wasn't the one who was human, but the *Stand-in Companion*. Yutori gazed vacantly at Hayato sipping his coffee with great relish. The transparent light streaming through from the rear window was forming just the right amount of shadow on his finely chiseled features.

Hayato didn't have a flamboyant personality, but he was serene and full of discretion. Even the furniture and tools he designed were devoid of any ostentation, but they all possessed a quiet gravitas about them.

Yutori was fond of the visuals the real Hayato, the graphic designer, created, but she also loved the many products Hayato the product designer created.

The real Hayato and the android Hayato.

The two of them were exactly the same Hayato.

From the day Hayato first arrived at the house in Tokyo Yutori never felt any discomfort; she was unable to. It was as if, she thought, my husband, who had been away on a business trip for a very long time, has at last come back from some faraway land where he couldn't be reached by telephone or email – that's how it truly felt.

Their lives, since then, went on the same as ever. The days that passed were such that, had the real Hayato been there with her, those days would have surely transpired indistinguishably, in an identical manner.

If there was a difference between the present Hayato and the previous Hayato, it was only in whether or not procreation was possible.

However, crucially, Yutori herself was infertile, so such talk about Hayato was meaningless.

I have a little over eight years remaining with him... Yutori would lately find herself thinking now and then.

The rental period granted for a *Stand-in Companion* was limited to ten years without the possibility of extension. Strictly speaking, the *Stand-in Programme* was put in place to promote the independence of people who have lost their beloved in an unexpected event, so there was no room for flexibility regarding the rental period.

One day, eight years from today, Hayato will reach a day when he will no longer wake up. The signal to deactivate a *Stand-in Android* was to be transmitted while they slept.

Even Yutori would not be informed of this exact day. It would simply turn out that one morning she would find Hayato motionless next to her. Then, on the following day, the repossession team of the Relief Committee would come over and collect him. That was that.

In the Artificial Intelligence (AI) circuitry of the *Stand-in Android*, the functionality for becoming aware, either through self-discovery or by learning from others, that he or she was an android was disabled. For instance, even if Yutori was to say to Hayato now, 'You are, in fact, a *Stand-in Companion*,' he would be incapable of understanding Yutori's words. For this reason, there was no way she could convey to him that there remained, in his life span, only a little more than eight years.

Of course, Hayato knew of the existence of the *Stand-in Android Programme*.

As a matter of fact, it was possible for a *Stand-in Android* to apply to rent another *Stand-in Android*. Since they had the same 'human rights' that humans had, the right to apply was only natural.

Say, for example, a man who has lost his wife, receives, on the grounds of his sorrow being unendurable, permission to rent a *Stand-in Companion*, but goes on to die three years later. Then, the bereaved *Stand-in Companion* must spend her remaining seven years as a widow. If she then wants to have a *Stand-in Companion* for the purpose of overcoming *her* own grief, she would be able to apply for one. And if approved, another *Stand-in Companion* would be dispatched to her.

5

For quite a while now, for the sake of exacting revenge, Hayato was beginning to consider living apart from Yutori.

The Yutori before him was none other than Yutori, but she was different in one decisive way. The real Yutori had betrayed Hayato badly, but this Yutori he was drinking coffee with now, while listening to Johann Strauss, would do no such thing.

Having been rented to heal Hayato's wound caused by the divorce, she would never leave him until the due date.

At the same time, Hayato, too, for a period of ten years, was unable to part from Yutori. It was a prerequisite of renting a *Stand-in Companion*.

There is something immeasurable about the damage to the human psyche when losing an irreplaceable partner. The loss of a partner has in many cases caused individuals to go on and ruin the rest of their lives. To prevent such tragedies, the *Stand-in Android Programme* was devised – employing the latest, cutting-edge androids.

The ten year rental period was set as it was considered the most suitable length of time for the bereaved to come to terms with the loss of a loved one. However, renters are required to get back on their feet within that time frame. But despite this, what it actually meant from society's perspective was that no *responsibility* towards grief-stricken individuals would be tolerated beyond this.

Eight years from now, the Yutori before him will cease to move.

Should Hayato, after waking up, call out to Yutori lying next to him, she will not utter a single word, nor will she give even the slightest response. Even if he shook her body or called her name out aloud, she, without ever opening her eyes, will not answer.

Such a morning will come suddenly.

Then, on the next day, the repossession team from the Relief Committee would come over and collect Yutori, now motionless. That would spell the end of his relationship with her.

When he applied for a *Stand-in Companion* he neither thought about nor imagined such a morning. All he hoped to do, in earnest, was to see to it that this person called Yutori would taste the same humiliation she made him taste; the same humiliation which, to him, was beyond belief. Any sentiments or emotions other than this impulse for revenge were frozen.

But spending two years together in this way, carrying on a married relationship, which in some ways never changed, Hayato's intense feelings gradually subsided.

It will be impossible for the two of us to have our own child, thought Hayato. It was this resignation, Hayato believed, that proved, in the end, to be the largest factor.

After all this time, Hayato now thought the kind of futile break-up they went through probably would never have occurred if he had only properly told the real Yutori, when they were living together, his honest feelings; for instance, he could have said, 'Why don't we give up on having a child now and simply think about our lives as just the two of us? If you still hope to bear a child anyway, there's the option of deciding to proceed with a divorce.'

When Hayato met Yutori, he was perplexed by how different she was from him in every possible way, from her way of thinking to her lifestyle. Nonetheless, guided by several unforeseen coincidences, he decided to marry her. But even then, the idea of having a child with her never occurred to him. He only hoped to share the rest of his life with Yutori, his wife.

For Yutori, a woman, it probably wasn't like that.

She certainly wanted to have a child, and Hayato naturally thought that, as a husband, it was his duty to help fulfill that wish together.

But even Yutori, in the first place, apparently didn't marry Hayato because she had wanted a child. At least, in the early days of their marriage, she didn't assume, Hayato believed, that being together with him was meaningless if they couldn't have children.

But ever since they began attempting, only to find out that there was a physical problem with Hayato, the look in her eyes had clearly changed.

That look, though, was absent in Yutori today.

On the contrary, she was feeling guilty and indebted to Hayato, believing that it was because of her infertility that they couldn't have a child, just as Hayato himself had felt guilty and indebted to her once.

If that's the case, there was no longer any need to continue taking revenge on her, was there?

Or rather, at the point of renting a *Stand-in Companion*, an entity incapable of bearing a child in the first place, this revenge game may have had already lost its significance.

Even Hayato couldn't come to grips with his own feelings, which kept changing.

Still, the notion that he had had enough was now firmly rooted deep inside his heart.

Eight years later, he would have to part from the Yutori in front of him.

On the morning he found Yutori in a sleep from which she would never awake, how on earth was he going to accept the reality of it?

Lately, he often thought about this eventuality.

At the time it happened, it would probably bring about a totally different sentiment from the one he experienced that day when Yutori left him. During the last year, the last several months, he would be conscious every single day, of parting from her, and no doubt, he would continue to brace himself, wondering when that morning would arrive.

While sharing the bed with a completely clueless Yutori, he would tightly embrace her warm body, secretly frightened that tonight might be the last night.

Then he would ask himself, until this night, how much was I able to do for her, how much happiness was I able to provide her?

By that time, the question of whether or not they had a child would, without doubt, not even cross the corner of his mind.

He would have no choice but to gaze at the sleeping face of his wife, pleasantly sleeping her usual way in the comfort of his arm and, within the emotion of fear, dread and apprehension, take stock of his calibre as a human.

6

Johann Strauss was over, and the music had changed.

Yutori was lost in thought while looking down, so she couldn't tell whether it was something that Hayato had requested.

'Shall we go now?' Hayato said after she looked up. His coffee cup had become empty before she knew it.

'Yes, why not?' Yutori drank up the rest of her coffee.

Just as she was about to stand up, though, Hayato murmured, 'Shall we stop taking hot-spring trips altogether?'

Yutori, who had half risen to her feet, sat down again.

'Instead,' he added timidly, 'why not go to some other places more, just as we used to when we got to know each other?'

'When we got to know each other?'

'Uh-huh.'

Come to think of it, Yutori recalled, around the time of their marriage, whenever they could both spare time off from work, they used to frequently set out abroad. But since the number of holidays that Yutori – an office worker – could take were limited, it was Hayato who always adjusted, working around her schedule, to make the trips feasible.

'You're not working now, Yutori, so, compared to those days, you're free to go to all sorts of places.'

'In that case…' Yutori said before stopping to study Hayato's manner; perhaps he wanted to give up on the hot-spring trips, which they had been going on for nearly two years, merely to try another way to achieve results.

You don't have to do anything like that anymore, Yutori whispered in her heart.

'In that case, I will accompany you to wherever you want to go. Because from now on I want you to live the way you want to live.'

Hayato returned her gaze with an expression of doubt and suspicion. 'Live the way I want to live?'

'That's right,' Yutori nodded. 'Because my number one wish is to be with you, as you live the life you design, the life you envisage, the life you fancy — the life you want.'

'Kazufumi Shiraishi is a unique writer. You can survey the contemporary literary scene in Japan, but I doubt you will readily find any author comparable to him.'

The Mainichi Shimbun

'Kazufumi Shiraishi is an ingenious author who writes with real flair and insight. In this compelling story he seamlessly blends the universal themes of love, loss and rivalry into a future world driven by cutting-edge technology and AI. This is a love story with a difference; one that will resonate with the reader in a thoroughly thought-provoking manner.'

Alex Pearl, author of *Sleeping with the Blackbirds*

'Kazufumi Shiraishi explores concepts of love, identity and place and the "why" of human existence.'

RTÉ

'Exceptionally well done... It's the most satisfying novel I've read in quite some time.'

The Complete Review, commenting on *The Part of Me That Isn't Broken Inside* by Kazufumi Shiraishi

Red Circle Minis

Original, Short and Compelling Reads

Red Circle Minis is a series of short captivating books by Japan's finest contemporary writers that brings the narratives and voices of Japan together as never before. Each book is a first edition written specifically for the series and is being published in English first.

The book covers in the series draw on traditional Japanese motifs and colours found in Japanese building, paper, garden and textile design. Everything, in fact, that is beautiful and refined, from kimonos to zen gardens and everything in between. The mark included on the covers incorporates the Japanese character *mame* meaning 'bean', a word that has many uses and connotations including all things miniature and adorable. The colour used on this cover is known as *torinoko-iro*.

 Red Circle

Showcasing Japan's Best Creative Writing

Red Circle Authors Limited is a specialist publishing company that publishes the works of a carefully selected and curated group of leading contemporary Japanese authors.

For more information on Red Circle, Japanese literature, and Red Circle authors, please visit:
www.redcircleauthors.com

Lightning Source UK Ltd.
Milton Keynes UK
UKHW011453290720
367363UK00002B/177